The Bioum Project

By David Evans

Table of Contents

Tricon was established twenty years ago in Washington Dc. Tricon is a top-secret company. Tricon has a thousand employees, each employee is given a special badge to be able to enter the facility.

The facility used to be located in San Diego California, but because of the recent seismic activity had to be moved to Washington DC. The research that is done in the laboratory is like nothing that you could imagine.

Nothing has ever gone wrong with the experiments that they have done. But recently the Tricon is working on researching more into artificial technology and robots. Tricon employees are well paid and have the best healthcare.

After the employees turn sixty-five years old they are able to retire. So far four employees have retired and are enjoying their lives.

As of lately though Tricon has been redoing the way it conducts its research. The facility is so top secret that there are guards who patrol the grounds of the facility day and night.

Everything about the facility is secret. To enter the facility there's a huge bullet resistant fence that opens and closes automatically.

On the corner of the fence is a camera, this camera is shock resistant and is waterproof. This camera controls itself and will automatically zoom in if it thinks there's a strange person trying to enter.

One day someone tried to breech the fence, the security guards took him down, he died in a struggle with the guards.

He was driving a semi-truck and had rammed it right into the fence, the fence is more like a wall than a fence.

The part of the wall, that was made of concrete had crumbled. By there are three walls that surround the facility. There are three guard towers with trained snipers in them.

Half of the facility is under the ground, there are five levels to the facility. The facility goes down three miles under the ground. The first floor is three miles below the ground, the first section is called the deep ground level.

The next level is called the Metrix, the third level is called Maxxer. The fourth level is called halfway above level, the top level is called the open-air level. The faculty has eight different sections; half of the sections are beneath the ground.

There's one main dining hall for the employees, and in between were the labs are located are offices. There are ten offices in total, the staff that work in the offices aren't permitted to be able to go into the labs.

This rule has recently been imposed on the employees. The scientists that work in the labs have several years of training in bio engineering. Each scientist is allowed to carry a pistol.

The pistol is a small caliber and is probably as powerful as a twenty-two bullet. The scientists feel that they are entitled to everything in the lab.

But some things in the lab the scientists can't access, a government agency from the pentagon hat has to come in to open the one cabinet that's located in the back of each lab.

The labs aren't too big in size, there's just enough room to work. The counter tops are all made of a special material that's germ free.

If a substance gets spilled on the countertop, it's in the regulations that it must be cleaned up right away. The scientists are careful not to spill anything on the counter tops, in each lab there are two magnifying microscopes.

There's a sink in each lab, and a box of orange rubber gloves. While the scientists are working in the lab they have to wear a pressurized disinfected suit. The suit kind of looks like an astronaut suit.

To take off the suit they have to unzip it and fold it up outside of the labs entrance. To get into any of the labs, the scientists have to swipe their badges and type in a four-digit code.

If the code is typed in wrong, then it'll make a loud beep and lock itself. Although this hasn't happened before, the floors of the labs have to be moped twice every day. The scientists aren't allowed to work in a dirty lab, there are two main cameras, in each laboratory.

These aren't no typical cameras; these cameras are equipped with night vision. They can turn in any direction, to monitor what the scientists are doing.

There are three main command centers, that are in the center level of the facility. In the command center rooms there are ten monitors, and a special escape hatch that leads down to the level below there.

There’s a small table in the command rooms, on top of the table is some extra walkie talkies for emergency purposes.

There are two generator rooms, in these rooms there are two generators. The generators are diesel and will only turn on if the power goes out. The generators would give half of the facility enough power to run for month. The power in the facility has gone out once before, the facility is open twenty-four seven. It took five years for this facility to be built.

Chapter 1: Envoi

The government hasn’t disclosed how much money it cost to finish the facility. The facility has one main room, for weapons. There are three different kind of weapons in the weapons lab room.

There are weapons that use rays of energy, then there are the weapons that shoot exploding bullets. Each weapon is very dangerous to use.

Nobody in the lab has had to use the weapons on anything or anyone. Some of the scientists get impatient with each other and get into arguments. Although their arguments don't last very long, they get back to work.

The scientists work from 10:30 am ‘until 9:30 pm, the scientists have plenty to do each day and like to keep busy.

Everybody that works in the facility is allowed to live there, each person lives in an ecological friendly mini apartment.

The apartments have everything that a person needs to live. There are two main elevators that are located in the center of the facility, there’s a large trail cart that leads up to the surface.

The train cart is made out of lightweight aluminum. The train cart is fast, its top speed is fifty miles per hour. It floats a few inches up off of the track, this makes it a smoother ride for the passengers.

If there would be an emergency, then the train cart would lock itself up. Most of the systems in the facility are completely automated.

The cameras are all equipped with a trip alarm, that'll go off if the cameras sees a fire or something suspicious happening.

All the cameras have facial recognition technology and know what every employee looks like.

When the scientists get into an argument and raise their voice at each other, the camera will briefly zoom in and listen to them. Then zoom back and go back to their regular duty. The scientists are so used to the cameras zooming in and out and watching them.

One time a scientist was working in the lab. He became so irritated with what he was doing, that the camera zoomed in on him.

He slammed the camera with his textbook, with all the force that he used, it didn't damage the camera.

He shook his head and thought to himself I'm tired of these cameras watching me. The camera then zoomed back in and stopped monitoring the scientist.

The scientists aren't allowed to eat any food in the laboratories and if they do then they're reported. On the second level of the facility there are fake city scenes, these scenes make it not seem like you're under the ground.

There are no windows in any of the levels except one at the top level. The scientists get tired from working and get sent back to their apartments to rest. The office workers and scientists get an hour break for lunch each day.

Although as of lately it's not been long enough for some of the employees. The employees don't have to leave the facility, if they do and get caught then they'll be fined a large sum of money. The facility has three highly secret rooms.

Each secret room has one guard who's armed, with an assault rifle who stands right outside the doorway. One of the three secret rooms is called the creature research laboratory.

The creatures that they have created are very dangerous and intelligent, there are six creatures, that are housed in this room. Each creature is a different size and has its own special attributes.

The one creature is as large as a leopard and the largest creature is six foot tall, each creature has a name. The creatures mainly remain calm but can't be trusted, there used to be more creatures. They since died, now there are just six of them.

None of these creatures has ever gotten out of its pen. There's an electric fence that surrounds the creatures, pens. Each creature has large sharp teeth, and sharp claws. The creatures have good eyesight and can sense, everything that happens in their surroundings.

The creatures make noises while they're awake. When the scientists walk into the room, the creatures look at them and growl. Then after a few minutes the creatures calm down and remain quiet.

The creatures are very ugly looking, there skin is a dark blackish color. They have some fur on their bodies, the creatures sometimes get anxious and walk around inside of their cages, and stare at the scientists.

There's one large desk in the middle of the room, there are two chairs on either side of the desk. The creatures have a strange smell to them, the creatures are given raw meat, twice each day.

If the creatures aren't given a meal twice a day then they go crazy and scream out. The creatures can make a screaming sound almost like a human.

There are three microscopes in the creature room, the creatures can recognize the scientists. The creatures are injected with a special serum to test how well their cells are growing.

Some of the creatures are dying because their cells just can't multiply quick enough to help heal their body.

One time one of the scientists that was working in the creature lab, he gave the one small creature too much meat. The creature swallowed the piece of meat, then choked on it.

The creature fell back on its back and started shaking, the creature then stood up and spit up a piece of meat. The piece of meat flew out of the cage, and landed on the scientist's paper that he was reading.

He was so horrified that he dropped his textbook that he was reading and ran out of the lab. Then another scientist had to come in and take over his job.

While the second secret room is called the water creature laboratory. In this laboratory there are four aquatic creatures.

Some of the four aquatic creatures try to jump out of the Aquariums, each water creature has sharp teeth.

Chapter 2: Human Testing

The scientists are careful not to put their hands near the aquarium, the creatures can swim around very quickly. Some of the creature's kind of resembled a piranha.

The scientists would wear protective welding gloves when they have to put something in the aquarium. The scientists had to mix up a certain kind of chemical and placed the chemical inside of a dropper.

Then they dropped the chemicals into the water, to see what certain chemicals would do to the water creatures.

The third secret room is where they do the human experiments. So far they have only experimented on three people.

The test subjects weren't happy with what they were put through. They experimented on two men, and one woman, the two men were six foot five and were thirty-two years old.

The women was forty-two years old and had one ponytail going down her back. They laid down the three people on a soft mattress and put a blind fold over their eyes and told them that it was going to be okay.

There arms and legs were tied down on custom metal rails that rose up from the mattress. The three people were told to remain still and relaxed, while the scientists got the special serum ready to inject into them. The women wasn't able to stay still for very long and her legs became restless and wouldn't stop shaking.

The scientists weren't sure what to do about the women's legs shaking. The one scientist walked over to the medicine cabinet and looked for a muscle relaxer medication.

He saw that there was a bottle of Aleve and Advil in the first drawer that he had opened. He looked in the next drawer, he found some blood thinner and some small diabetic needles.

He still couldn't find what he was looking for, so he looked in the last drawer, this drawer had some papers folded up in it.

The papers mentioned about how the experiments on the people should be performed. There were a bunch of yellow post it notes all over the paperwork. The paperwork was turning yellow from being in the drawer for so long.

The scientist reached through the drawer and finally found a muscle relaxer. He opened the bottle and took out two muscle relaxers.

He didn't even take the time to look at the milligrams of how many he should give to the women.

He placed the two pills on the sterol countertop and took off his gloves and put on another pair. The two men had fallen asleep, but the women was still acting hyper.

The one scientist looked at the other and said do you think that we should give the women the muscle relaxer now or wait? The other scientist eyes brows lifted up, he said I don't see why not.

One of the scientists took out a paper cup and filled it with some kind of mineral water. The women's eyes weren’t closed, she still wasn’t relaxed. The scientist had her sit up and gave her two pills with the mineral water.

The women's name is Mackenzie, both men's names are Jack and Zac. The two scientist’s names who are working in the human testing lab are Bradley and Butch.

“Do you think that Mackenzie will be better after the relaxer pills?”

“Yes,” I do well it seems like she has calmed down and her legs stopped shaking.

“How’s the mixing process coming along?”

“It's going just swell, but some of the special blue DNA isn’t combining itself with the green DNA. “

“Do you know why that is?”

“No,” I don't, you better be able to help me to fix it, or we might lose our jobs.

No, we aren’t going to lose our jobs, let's just not make any mistakes. Remember that we have to look at the RNA and DNA under the microscope.

Now stay steady, you can’t drop a single vile on the floor or we could be fired and worse turn into something from the poisonous green DNA.

We need to make a lot of progress on our experiments each day, I realize that you and I work well together.

"Have you looked at the strains of green DNA under a microscope yet?"

"Yes," I have been trying to get the green DNA cells to multiply and this will then make the strain of DNA complete.

We need to be able to make the DNA evolutionize to complete the experiment. I don't want you to inject the patients anymore.

"Why not?"

"The other day you slipped and almost dropped a syringe full of DNA and that was lousy."

"Why don't you give me a second chance?"

"Listen I don't give second chances; okay I see how you want to be then. I'm going to keep my mouth shut and do my work and try to stay away from you."

"Did you inject the women yet with the pink cells?"

"No," but I'm about to do that, so hold on.

"Your hands and arms are trembling, are you going to be okay?"

"Yes," I'll be fine.

"How are you going stick her with the needle when you are shaking so much?"

Don't worry sometimes my hands tremble, but eventually they'll stop shaking. See that they stopped shaking already, only ten minutes have gone by.

You know that were ahead of schedule on our research and that's a good thing. Now I'm going to stick the women with the needle, alright now be careful. I'll be careful.

The woman is resting, I hope she doesn't get upset with me. After I'm done poking her with the needle, Bradley slowly walked over close by the women and sat down on the wheeled chair.

He brought over the rubbing alcohol to prep the area of where the needle was going to be placed into her arm.

He carefully pulled up her gown and her whole arm was now exposed; the women didn't seem to move or stir at all. She must have fallen asleep or so they thought.

"Would you hurry up"

"Why should I hurry up and hurt her, we got plenty of time to get all of our research done?"

"Don't try to hurry me again"

"Do you understand me?"

"Yes"

Bradley was careful not to disturb the women who was lying on asleep on the operating table. Come on Bradley don't be shy and inject the women, with the last bit of serum that's left.

Chapter 3: Assault

Okay but if she dies it's on going to be on you, she isn't going to die. Suddenly the women jumped up and bit down into Bradley's arm.

With a swift punch using his hand, he hit the women square in the face. She let go of his arm and went back to sleep, blood went running down his arm. She bit me and now my arm is a bloody mess.

“Could you please help me, yes give me a moment to get the bandages ready?”

“Listen to me I think that the women has gone crazy. I can't believe that she just bit my arm.”

“Do you think that she’s a zombie?”

“No,” I don't think so

My whole left arm is swelling up and burns, she had sharp teeth to pierce into my flesh like she did.

Now let me bandage your arm, but you must stay still. I know that it hurts but you have to just deal with it for now, your face is beginning to get all pale white. I’m getting concerned that you’re going to faint.

“Do you feel yourself?”

“Yes, but my arm just burns and aches.”

That feeling will go away soon enough, look out the women is standing up behind you. The women ran over and tried to bite into Bradley's throat.

Stop her, she got me good now. The women bit into the side of his throat and blood came squirting out of his throat and women continued to bite his throat.

Bradley fell over and pool of blood encompassed his body, butch was frozen in fear and did nothing to protect himself.

The women bend down and began to rip out Bradley's intestines from his belly. She kept on munching on his dead body, Butch tried to run but she grabbed onto his leg, and he fell.

He took a bite out of his left sneaker. He attempted to get up and slipped and fell again, this time he fell onto his face and broke his nose.

The women climbed on top of him, and he fainted. She bit off several fingers on his hand, then left him go.

Butch didn't wake up, and there was blood all over the floor by where Butches body laid. The crazy women went on feasting on Bradley's dead body.

In the command room, Swegert was monitoring the cameras. He saw what was happening in the one lab where the crazy women was.

He set off the alarm, three armed guards went running down the main hallway, and ran towards the lab.

It took them so long to get into the lab, the door was jammed and didn't open. One of the guards tried his key but it didn't work.

All three guards kicked the door at once and it fell in, the crazy women was growling at them like a wild dog.

She ran towards the three guards and they shot her to death, the three guards checked for a pulse on Bradley and Butch.

Butch still had a weak pulse, but Bradley no longer had a pulse and was dead. Suddenly Bradley's body became reanimated, he stood up and began to snarl and growl like a wild dog.

He too ran at the three guards, they shot him to death. Butch's body remained motionless on the floor.

The blood on the floor made the floor so very slipperily. One of the guards tripped and fell onto the body of the dead woman.

It made him so terrified that he left the two other guards behind and ran back to his office. The two remaining guards didn't seem to know what to do without their leader.

They took Butches body with them and exited the room, they made sure to close the door behind them. They carried Butches body down the hallway and were getting out of breath.

They let Butches body drop down onto the floor and left his body there and walked on. They didn't seem to care where they left the body.

They went back to the guard's office and relaxed in their comfy office chairs. Swegert looked into the five television screens and saw that the guards didn't do their jobs.

They had left a body in the hallway, he put on his hat and walked out of the command center to check out what was going on. He ran over to the guard's office and ripped open the door, I've been watching you on the cameras.

> "Why did you drop the body in the hallway?"
>
> "His body was heavy, so we had to put his body down."
>
> "Are you guys just afraid to break a sweat or what?"
>
> "No," then get back out there and pick up his body again, okay we will now don't worry.

You guys better do what I just said, or you guys will be relieved of your duties.

> "Is that understood"
>
> "Yes Sir."

Swegert left the guards office and slammed the door with all his strength. He slowly walked back to the command center and sat down in the comfy office chair.

He looked into the bottom left television and saw that in lab two another patient had gone crazy. They began to attack the Drs. who were in the room, Swegert couldn't believe his eyes and kept his eyes glued to the screen.

The alarm went off and the guards were sent out too stop another attack that was going on. But this attack was far worse than the attack that happened earlier that day. This time there was a crazy man that was chasing the Drs. all around the lab.

He mauled one of the Drs. and bit into his left arm, then the crazy man jumped on the other Drs. who were in the room and were beginning to bite them.

The Drs couldn't stop the crazy man, he kept on getting a hold of them. This time the crazy man killed three Drs. and began to devour their dead bodies.

At this point Swegert didn't know what to do. He was so scared that he thought about locking himself in the security room.

He heard a scream coming from one of the labs, he happened to look at one of the television screens.

He saw that there was a woman running down a long hallway with one of the zombie Drs. chasing after her.

He couldn't believe his eyes, the zombie Dr. was so fast that he grabbed a hold of the women who was still screaming and bit into her throat, blood squirted out all over the wall behind her.

Chapter 4: Do or Die

Then her lifeless body collapsed onto the floor where there was a pool of blood. The zombie Dr. bent over and began to eat her body.

There was blood all over his chin, he let out a fierce roar. Something must have disturbed him, he stood back up and looked through the window at Swegert.

Swegert was frozen in fear and the zombie Dr. starred into his eyes. Swegert quickly looked away, the zombie Dr slammed himself against the door.

Luckily the door was good and locked. Swegert grabbed a screwdriver off of his desk and clenched it tightly in his sweaty hands.

Go ahead you crazy zombie, I'm going to stop you if you break the door down. A few minutes later he got tired of holding onto the screwdriver and put it back down on the desk in front of him.

The zombie Dr. soon grew tired of trying to break the door down and gave up and lumbered down the long hall. He tripped over his own foot and fell face down, onto the floor. He let out a moan and remained on the floor motionless.

Swegert looked up at the television screen and saw that the zombie Dr. who was in the hallway had fallen down and remained there motionless. He looked over towards his left, and looked into the television screen that was off to his left.

He saw two zombies lumbering along in the hallway that led to the cafeteria, the door to the cafeteria was open and there were bloody fingerprints all over the cafeteria door.

Three zombies came lumbering out of the entrance to the cafeteria, blood was running down all of their faces.

All of the zombies began to moan and groan, one of the zombies walked into another zombie and let out a groan.

Both zombies fell onto the ground, they were so weak neither one of them could get up again. After Swegert saw this he broke into the cabinet to the right of him and took out pistol and a shotgun.

The Shotgun was a twelve gauge with buck shot, the pistol was a 454 and was fully loaded and so was the shotgun.

He swung open the door and began to walk down the hallway, immediately the zombies smelled him and came running.

Two zombies came around the corner, he shot one zombie in the head. His brain exploded all over the place.

While the other zombie came on coming closer, he shot this zombie with the 454 pistol and made a perfect shot.

He hit the zombie right between the eyes, but the pistol kicked back so hard that it sprained his right wrist.

Two more zombies came walking along, he quickly pumped the shotgun and shot both of the zombies at the same time. Both their heads were blown off and they dead bodies fell onto the floor.

Swegert walked down the hallway back to the control room and slammed the door shut, locking it. Once he sat down, he looked at the television screen that showed the cafeteria and made the camera zoom in.

There were ten zombies just slowly lumbering along, one of the zombies was chewing on another zombies left arm. Another zombie was dragging something with him. He looked closer and saw that he was dragging along another zombie who was missing half of his body.

There was blood all over the white tile floor. There was one zombie in particular and this zombie was so different than the rest of the zombies. His face was all red and so was the rest of the body.

Suddenly he bent over and changed into a devil creature, he walked on four legs like a dog. He jumped up and grabbed a hold of the other zombies and began to rip them apart.

He tore up all of the zombies in the room and collapsed onto the floor and stopped moving. Swegert couldn't believe what he was witnessing.

Suddenly a man came into the room and put a gun to the back of Swegert head. Excuse me Swegert, Yes Sir.

Please shut down the facility right now, that's a direct order. I'm going to pull the trigger anyway; bang and the gun went off and Swegerts brains were all over the television screens.

The strange man sat in Swegerts seat and shot out all of the television monitors then shot himself in the head. Jack and Zac were hiding in the safe room on the fourth floor, we're not going to be safe here for much longer.

Were in the room next to the secret room, I hope there's no monsters in there. I'm afraid all the staff have turned into those things by now.

I can't imagine what the water creatures are doing unsupervised, they're probably fighting with the things.

If the water creatures come out of the water, their bodies will grow arms and legs and they'll begin walking upright.

I surely would like to know what was in those special serums, I know how we can find out if we go to the lab on the third floor. There's no way I'm going with you down there, you'll never make it back up here.

You're not so good at defending yourself, I thought for sure one of those things was going to eat you.

"Do you think any of the guards are alive?"

"No."

"Do you think those things can communicate with one another?"

"No."

I can't stand the fact that we're trapped in here, it's just how it is. We should be in one of the labs trying to make an antidote instead of sitting up here just talking.

Those labs are probably teaming with those things, I doubt those things are in every lab. You should have taken the dead guards gun; I at least have a steel bar. We can always find another weapon along the way.

You still have a little bit of panic in your eyes, you would to after what we went through. I don't want to become like one of those things and become brain dead and be stuck in this place forever. After you and I get out of this place, we'll call the authorities and tell them to demolish this place. A sudden banging sound alerted them; I hope that it's not one of those things trying to get in here.

It sounds to me like it's coming from the secret room, they heard the sound several more times. Whenever it is sounds like it really wants to get out of where it is. I'd go investigate but I'm too afraid of what it might be.

With my luck I would go out there and one of the things to come after me. I can barely see anything through this window over here.

"Did you see anything coming out of the secret room yet?"

"No."

So far I don't see anything in the hallway, the coast looks clear for now. They heard a loud blast, look there's something coming out of there.

It looks like a humanoid robot; another one just came out. They never told us that they were working on robotics.

Chapter 5: Panic

Then a third robot came out, I wonder what caused them to wake up now. It's probably because I pressed in the emergency button earlier.

"Do you think they're going to hurt us?"

"No."

They're probably looking for the threat, I'm sure they're going to kill those things.

"Should we follow them?"

“No,” we don't want to interfere with what they're doing.

I wonder if they have the smarts to know the passcodes. I'm sure it was programmed into their software; they heard a rustling sound above them; part of the ceiling fell in and there was a man lying there.

He had a terrified look on his face and couldn't get a word out. I barely got out of my office alive, when I opened my door those things were everywhere in the hallway.

I quickly slammed my door shut and got up on my chair. I was able to break through the ceiling tile and got myself up in the duct work.

I didn't have any idea where it led to, I had happened to look down and those things broke through my door.

“Did you see if they were communicating with one another?”

“No.”

There was blood all over their bodies, one of them was missing both its arms and walked awfully wobbly.

“How many of them broke in your room?”

“Three of them.”

They were sniffing around the room for my sent. One of them tore into the other ones neck, they're not fond of one another.

"What do you know about the secret room over here?"

"I know what they have in there."

We just witnessed what was in there come out of there.

"Were you surprised about what you saw?"

"Yes," we thought that there more of those things in there.

"How long ago did they begin working on the research on them?"

"Three years ago."

"Did you help them with the research?"

"Yes," just for several months.

These are the fifth kind of prototype humanoid robots; the former robots were just left after they failed there tests.

"Do these robots have weapons?"

"Yes," multiple one's.

"If something goes wrong will they self-destruct?"

"No."

"How long have the both of you been up here?"

"For two hours."

"What kind of weapons do the robots have?"

"Ray guns, machine guns, and flash bang grenades."

"Have the robots ever gone after each other?"

"No."

They know every nook and cranny in this facility.

"Will they take us as hostages?"

"No."

Each one of the robots costs fifty thousand dollars, these machines have a twenty-year guarantee. They have facial recognition and can tell if you're happy or sad just by looking at you.

If you hold a gun up to them they'll shoot you. They'll shoot what there laser points to, while they were talking the leader of the zombies was getting his horde together to fight the roving robots. The zombie wasn't anticipating that the water creatures would also come after them.

Some of the robots were ready to fight the horde of zombies but they were just waiting for the zombie's leader to open the fire.

The leader had no idea about the gun so he threw it and raised his right hand as a gesture for his horde to attack the robots.

Zombies started lumbering toward robots and did their best to break their metallic bodies. Some of them were trying to pierce their pointed teeth inside the necks of the robots but they couldn't even scratch them.

Those robots were the best and the most advanced creation of Tricon. On the other hand, the aquatic creatures were left unsupervised.

They had started feeling hungry and were going mad. They were striking the glass walls of the aquarium but the aquarium was not made of ordinary glass.

The water creatures started to fight with one another and one of the creatures threw another one out of the aquarium. Consequently, the creature that came out of the aquarium collided with the flasks filled with the chemicals.

The rack that was full of beakers and test tubes having dangerous chemicals, fell down. The reagent's bottles and other containers bore a fall and shattered into pieces. The chemicals in the bottles and containers spilled on the ground and they came into reaction.

This chemical composition had never been thought of and was never mentioned in any book of chemical studies.

As a result of the composition reaction between those random chemicals. A green chemical was formed which was so volatile, that it was immediately converted into green fumes.

The fumes were purely poisonous, they started spreading around the lab. As soon as the fumes came into reaction with water in the aquarium, a blast blew the whole lab, and its highly protected door.

The other dozens of chemical bottles broke and they formed other toxic chemicals and unknown poisonous gases.

The aquatic creatures died due to the intense blast and the chemicals and fumes started spreading throughout the facility via vents.

Zac and Jack had heard the blast and they decided to come out and see what was happening around them. They saw a strange green gas coming out of one of the vents in the hallway.

It had a pricking and unbearable odor. They brought out their handkerchiefs and put them on their noses. But they couldn't stop them from going inside their nostrils, they started sneezing and coughing.

It felt like something was cutting their throats and their lungs were burning, they freaked out and started running here and there. Their eyes were red and watery and their noses started bleeding.

After a few minutes, their lungs stopped working due to which they lost their breath and consequently their lives too.

Chapter 6: Robots Plans

The Zombies who were lumbering here and there were also freaked out due to the toxic fumes. The doctors and other staff, who were hiding from the zombies.

Weren't able to hide from the gas coming out of the vents. Since all the ducts were connected and the fans inside the ducts, were blowing the green gas from one place to another.

Doctors had turned on the alarms, they even tried to alert everybody to use safety masks. Those fumes had never been formed before, and thus no mask could stop them. The guard patrolling the grounds of the facility, had no idea what was going on inside the building.

Since the facility was soundproof and top secret. The guards were still on their duties, who were wandering around the main gates and the vast area around the facility.

The facility was facing a disaster that it had never faced. Only the creatures that weren't harmed inside the facility were the robots. They were so intelligent that they realized the reason behind the deaths.

They knew the gases won't harm them but the liquid chemicals could melt their metallic bodies. One of the robots went to a lab and called every robot in the hallway. The robots started to gather in the hallway.

Some of them, who were fighting with some of the zombies, killed the zombies before the fumes could get them.

The remaining zombies died due to the toxic fumes. Water creatures had already died and within fifteen minutes all the robots were gathered in the hallway.

"Okay, we're the only thing left here. We should choose a leader among ourselves who could lead us to establish this place again."

"Yes," we want a leader.

"Why not you become one?"

"Let's start working."

Get yourself divided into teams of three and spread on every level to gather every dead body from the facility. Then start with the clean-up process."

The robot who had become the leader reached into the secret lab, that had blueprints and documents of robots.

He went through those blueprints and attached himself with the cable that was used to program the robot.

He started reprogramming himself, stuffing himself with all information available on the internet. Soon his system ran out of storage space and he started twitching.

He quickly unplugged himself and went through the documents, he found out how he could get more storage space.

The lockers inside the lab had storage devices, that were capable of increasing the space up to hundreds of Terabytes.

The leader robot was having difficulty moving but he was already built on advanced technology. He used the information to break the locker code, and he opened it successfully after a few attempts.

He took out those mini chips having TBs of space and installed them inside his forehead by following a certain method explained in the documents.

After a few hours, he had become the most advanced robot in the world. Who had every piece of knowledge that was available on the internet.

The rest of the robots had finished their work and had gathered all the dead bodies of the humans and zombies in separate labs.

The facility had gotten a new life but without any humans. The leader decided to expose the new Tricon to the guards, and thus he went outside to let them see the new boss they would be working for.

The guards were shocked but they couldn't do anything since they knew. Tricon's scientist had something secret inside the building and it was no wonder that the robot they had created could do anything. Tricon was now a facility where the robots were the ones carrying out scientific research. The guards spread this exclusive news everywhere, that Tricon was now being handled by robots.

The government tried to contact the CEO and other officials but they had already died. The call from the government bodies was picked up by the leader robot.

The humans were ultimately shocked to hear a robot really handling the company where he was manufactured. The government set an appointment with the leader robot to know what they were up to.

They sent an expert AI scientist, Joy, to talk to the robot. "So, Mr. Leader, we all want to know your next steps and the medium of your upcoming research."

"We wil continue the work of our creators"

"If you want, we can provide you with a human leader."

"No, we don't want."

"Okay.”

“Can we send our best scientists here to help you?"

"No,” we can do everything on our own.

"You would have to sign this contract in which you have to agree that you won't conduct any illegal research here. Else the whole company will be taken from you." "We’ll do what we want, you can't even arrest us. You may leave.

“The leader robot had realized that humans were a serious threat to them, the zombies didn't even know what a gun was. The robot decided to do research on the zombies and turn every human on the planet into a zombie.

So that they’ll rule the world forever because the zombies had no brains to stand against the robots. On the other hand, Joy had a feeling that robots had gone out of control.

They called a team of top intelligent individuals to get the Tricon back from the possession of the robots. Joy and another secret intelligence officer Liam set up another appointment with the leader. They had a plan in their minds.

While they were having a usual chat with the leader they pretended to fight with one another. Joy intentionally hit Liam's nose so hard that it started bleeding, that was what they wanted.

The leader robot ordered his worker robots to take Liam to the lab where they had some bandages there for human dead bodies. Liam was exploring and watching everything closely while going toward the lab.

The lab where the robot took him was full of dead doctors and staff members. Some of the robots were working there.

One of them handed Liam a cotton bud, masking tape, and some spirit. On the other hand, Joy asked the leader robot to go to the washroom.

He had already seen the vents and decided to use them to find out their secret lab. He went into the washroom and found a vent there.

He took out his shoes and without making any sounds, worked with his pointed ring to open the vent. He successfully entered the vent and closed it so that nobody could get an idea about him escaping through it.

He crawled through the vent and checked every opening. He reached the lab where the robots were experimenting on the bodies of the zombies.

Liam got chills, he thought that robots had created zombies. He traveled back to the washroom and came out.

Chapter 7: Complete

Liam and Joy couldn't find out what exactly the robots were up to. They had a clue that the robots had something to do with the zombies. Now it had become much more important to stop them.

Joy and Liam called another meeting of intelligent scientists and agents. It took two weeks to come up with a plan through which they could stop the robots.

They tried to set up another meeting but the leader robot didn't allow them to enter the facility since they had almost completed their research and had prepared a vaccine.

That could be injected into the fields under irrigation, so that it gave out the crops that could turn any human into the zombie who eats it.

Liam and Joy talked to the guards patrolling around the facility. They told them that the building had some vents opening in the back.

Joy and Liam turned themselves into guards by putting on guards' uniforms and reached the back of the building. They entered the vent and traveled through them from level to level.

It took them a whole day to reach the secret lab since the vent had fans installed in the middle and it was hard to cross the fans. The secret lab was empty and locked since only the leader robot used to visit that lab.

The cameras in the lab were also not working. Liam and Joy read the documents of the robots and Joy, who was an AI scientist.

Had written a virus program that was able to erase every data stored in the robot. Joy installed that virus program in the machine placed in the lab through which the robots were programmed.

Now they just needed to bring the leader robot to the secret lab. Liam opened the lab from inside that started an alarm.

The leader robot rushed towards the lab without calling for other robots since he had sensitive data in the lab. When the robot saw Joy standing in the lab he took out his weapons but he couldn't shoot him.

Since he was standing behind the machine the data was stored in. Liam, who was hiding behind the lab's door holding the cable, quickly came out and attached the cable to the robot.

As soon as the cable was attached to the robot, the virus was installed in the robot's hardware within nanoseconds and it erased every piece of data. The leader robot stopped where he was standing.

Joy installed another simple program in which the only thing the robot needed to do was to order other robots to shut down on their own. After successfully saving the world from the zombie apocalypse.

Liam and Joy lay on the ground since they were so tired. The world was safe and it was proved that robots can be intelligent but not more than humans.

www.ingramcontent.com/pod-product-compliance
Lightning Source LLC
LaVergne TN
LVHW052108160826
845678LV00015B/3433

* 9 7 9 8 8 4 4 6 0 9 9 2 3 *